Monologues and Dialogues about
ORDINARY PEOPLE-
Extraordinary
GOD

Nameless men and women in the Bible who did amazing acts for the Kingdom of God

Written by Michael E. Owens
Illustrations by Leda Owens

Illustrations by Leda Owens

Ordinary People – Extraordinary God
Volume 1

Published by

Scribblers Press

9741 SE 174th Place Road, Summerfield, Florida 34491

Printed by

Trinity Press

3190 Reps Miller Road, Suite 360, Norcross, Georgia 30071

Cover design and illustrations by Leda Owens

Text set in Times New Roman

Printed in U.S.A.

Library of Congress Control Number:2019911827

Owens, Michael E., 08/05/2019

Ordinary People- Extraordinary God, Volume 1 / Michael E. Owens

Summary: A book of monologues and dialogues of stories of unnamed individuals in the Bible

ISBN: 978-1-950308-98-9

Table of Contents

Introduction

This is a book in a series of monologues and dialogues of various Bible characters – men and women - who have remained nameless through the centuries. These discourses are designed to be performed in Bible costumes in front of congregations of believers and non-believers. Before I thought of writing a book about these characters, I often though about these people and wondered who they were, what brought them to this moment in their lives and how this encounter with God changed their very being. I wished to know about their lives, their livelihood, their families, their views, how they felt as well as what happened to them after their encounter with God. These stories are not found in the Bible, but rather they are assumptions of what might have occurred with each of these special people. I rather see these stories as what I call "Sanctified Imaginations". I have tried to give a voice and a life to each of the individuals. Of course, there can be, and there are, many opinions and views about these personalities. I don't argue the point. Your ideas may be very different from mine, and that's fine. Use this book to spur your own imagination if you want; or use what is within these pages to tell the wonderful stories of these unique and exceptional, unnamed people of God.

When I tell these stories, I always do it with an appropriate costume that matches the character I am portraying. In each section of the book, you will find different costuming ideas. For the most part, these were very average people and their clothes reflected their status in the community – very plain and unassuming. I have included a few of commercial patterns that can be purchased to help in the construction of the various costumes.

I do not use a script while I am performing. I review the story often and tell it from the heart. There may be opportunity to add or even delete parts of the play. Use your own prayerful edition of these characters you will be portraying. Each story points to the saving grace of Jesus Christ. Make that the emphasis of each story you tell - that, through the Holy Spirit, every event and character you speak of will glorify God and His Son. Every play you perform is designed to lead people to personal salvation or to lead them into a deeper relationship with Christ. Plan that in each performance.

I would challenge you to study the Bible and find other nameless characters who have done amazing actions for the Kingdom and perform their story as well. Volume 2 contains several women parts, and Volume 3 will have more of a mix of male and female presentations.

Listen for the podcast of all the characters in the "Ordinary People – Extraordinary God" series with "The Mike and Friends Too Show" coming soon. Mike will present each dialogue and monologue and you can listen how Mike interprets each one. Hopefully this will help you in your presentations.

I pray that as you use this book, you will be blessed to see the fruit of your ministering through drama.

Acknowledgements

Many pastors and friends have been influential in the writing of this book. Their sermons as well as their informal discussions with me, have given me a deeper insight into the characters included in this book. I have appreciated their patience and interest in my project. They have shared their sermon notes, their time and their blessing to advance my work. For this, I am eternally grateful.

Specifically, I want to thank a few of them for their help. First and foremost, I want to thank my dearest friend, Danny Hawthorne, the former pastor of Agape Church in West Monroe, Louisiana. Now, the current pastor of Green Acres Baptist Church in Bastrop, Louisiana. Danny and I have been friends since undergraduate days at Louisiana College in Pineville, Louisiana, where we both received our bachelor's degrees. Danny had already committed to the ministry and was pursuing his life work of being a pastor. I was very honored to be with Danny as he celebrated his 50th year in the ministry in 2018. Over the years we were fortunate to be able to work together in several churches and other ministries. He was either the Youth Director or Pastor and I worked alongside him as the Music Minister. For several years we worked together at the Louisiana Correctional Institute for Women located in St. Gabriel, Louisiana under the direction of the ministry's founder, Mrs. Thelma Hebert and her daughter Karen. Danny has always been an inspiration to me through the years for his love of the Lord's work and his dedication to His church and His people. Danny and his wife, Meda as well as his children, Juliann, Jarrod, Jill, and Jayme have been a blessing and an encouragement to me throughout my life.

Additionally, there are other pastors and ministers who have influenced me in this endeavor.

Reverend Leland Hodges, pastor of Destiny International Church in Denham Springs, Louisiana was the first pastor for my wife and I right after we married. His sermons were clear, simple to understand, yet profound in their revelation of Truth from God's Word. It was here I was first able to use my gift for drama and storytelling. Bonnie and I performed the skit "The Innkeeper and His Wife" for the congregation; a skit included in this book. Over the years, I was able to write and perform other monologues that I have included here, including "The Owner of the Upper Room". I have been so thankful to Reverend Hodges' for his trust in me to tell God's stories through these skits.

Reverend Preston Thompson, pastor of the Redeemer Baptist Church in Baton Rouge, Louisiana became a dear friend and advisor for several years. He was my pastor during the time of my late wife's death. His comforting nature as well as those in our congregation helped me through a very difficult time. Bonnie and I were very blessed to be under his ministry. His sermons provided me a thorough and deepened understanding of scripture and I gleaned much about many of the characters in this book. I performed "The Sailor on the Ship with Jonah" at the church's school, Riverdale Christian Academy. I also wrote scripts for the Children's

Ministry's Christmas programs over the years.

Currently, my wife, Leda and I attend Parkview Church in Lilburn, Georgia, less than 5 minutes from our home. The interim pastor was Reverend Terry Gyger, a wonderful minister who presented the Word with grace and calm assurance. Although we have attended the church for less than a year, I have learned much from his sermons, which often encompassed tales of interesting characters. His stories not only contain thought-provoking insights into the who, what, when and where, but he can connect these individuals to the salvation story and how we can serve Christ, each other and the community. He has helped me connect the characters in my stories to the invitation to accept Jesus as Lord and Savior and to encourage His children to be faithful in His service.

Dedication

To my wife, Leda, whose patience, encouragement and
unwavering love
has kept me going in this endeavor

BOY WITH FIVE LOAVES AND TWO FISHES

Costume(s) for Boy with Five Loaves and Two Fishes

This costume would be better for a younger performer.

This costume would be better for a younger performer as well.

This costume would be better for an older performer.

Boy with Five Loaves and Two Fishes – John 6:1-14

The Scripture:

[1] Sometime after this, Jesus crossed to the far shore of the Sea of Galilee (that is, the Sea of Tiberias),

[2] and a great crowd of people followed Him because they saw the signs He had performed by healing the sick.

[3] Then Jesus went up on a mountainside and sat down with His disciples.

[4] The Jewish Passover Festival was near.

[5] When Jesus looked up and saw a great crowd coming toward him, He said to Philip, "Where shall we buy bread for these people to eat?"

[6] He asked this only to test him, for He already had in mind what He was going to do.

[7] Philip answered Him, "It would take more than half a year's wages to buy enough bread for each one to have a bite!"

[8] Another of his disciples, Andrew, Simon Peter's brother, spoke up,

[9] "Here is a boy with five small barley loaves and two small fish, but how far will they go among so many?"

[10] Jesus said, "Have the people sit down." There was plenty of grass in that place, and they sat down (about five thousand men were there).

[11] Jesus then took the loaves, gave thanks, and distributed to those who were seated as much as they wanted. He did the same with the fish.

[12] When they had all had enough to eat, He said to his disciples, "Gather the pieces that are left over. Let nothing be wasted."

[13] So they gathered them and filled twelve baskets with the pieces of the five barley loaves left over by those who had eaten.

[14] After the people saw the sign Jesus performed, they began to say, "Surely this is the Prophet who is to come into the world." *(NIV)*

The Preparation:

COSTUME – Simple costume with turban that is like other characters in the book like a shepherd, inn keeper, or one of the four who helped the paraplegic. If performed by a young person, the costume should be shorter perhaps, and no head piece would be required.

AGE – Any age could perform this character. If a young person, state that this event happened recently.

BACKGROUND – This was probably a lad from a poor family. The parents must have needed to stay behind to care for their home, family members, etc.

DEMEANOR – Amazement and wonderment. He still can't believe such a miracle could happen.

The Story:

Can you believe? *(laughing excitedly.)* That 'young lad' was me! Yes, me! Many years ago. I cannot tell you how many times I have told that story. I am not a boy anymore. Now I am an old man. But I remember that story as if it happened yesterday. I must take you back many, many years ago. *(Pause)* I had heard of Jesus, and I had heard of His miracles. At the time, I didn't believe them. But I was very curious. At first my mother argued with me about going to see this Jesus.

"You are too young to travel around the hillsides," she told me.

"But mother," I said back to her, "I've taken the sheep there many times and back, and I was very safe." Of course, I did not mention the threat of wild animals I could have encountered. If I had done that, Whoa! She would have never let me go again. I watched her eyes and I could see a hesitation there. Now was my time to convince her.

"But father knows I have been to those hills before," I pleaded. "He doesn't see anything wrong." Of course, he had said the same thing my mother was saying, but I had won him over. Now just to persuade her. I watched her pause then make a big sigh. I got her!

"Okay," she said reluctantly, "but you must take a lunch and be back before dark. You promise?" What do you think I said?

"Yes," I answered. I then waited for her as she placed some small fish she had been drying in the sun and a few loaves of bread she had just baked in a basket. I slung the long cord of the basket over my shoulder and I was out the door.

I was so excited and a little scared to be traveling to the hills. Had I been there before? Oh, yes. I didn't lie. But just to the edge of those hills, and always with someone with me as I tended the sheep. This time I was alone. But soon, there were many more who had joined ME, traveling to see Jesus.

As I walked along with the others, I could hear them speak about this man named Jesus.

"He made the lame to walk," said one. "My friend was blind, but now he can see!" exclaimed another. "He was your friend?" called out another. "Well," the man answered, "he was a friend of a friend who was a cousin, I believe. But he can see now!"

I wasn't sure who or what to believe. I wanted to find out for myself.

I'm not sure I had ever seen so many people in one place before in my life. It looked like hundreds and hundreds, maybe even thousands. I couldn't count that high.

As I viewed the huge throngs of people, I was pushed along as they massed together, being squeezed one way and another. I couldn't see anything. I was small and the others were much taller. I was beginning to feel as if I had made a mistake coming here. There was nothing I could do but let the crowd move me along. I was about to give up and head for home, as it was now getting late. I pushed hard to go the other way, but I couldn't fight the crowd. Then, *(pause)* an eerie silence came over the crowd and the jostling soon stilled, and I began to see people around me settling down. In a moment, I was alone as I stood there. I was facing a sea of people looking right past me. Then I felt a tug on my clothes. I looked down and a woman sitting in front of me was pulling on my tunic. I didn't understand at first, until I glanced across the grassy fields and everyone was seated. When I turned around, there He was – right before me. *(begin looking down and raise eyes slowly to where Jesus would be standing)* The woman tugged again, only this time harder and she yanked me to the ground. She yanked so hard; my lunch fell out of my basket on to the grass. I scurried to pick up the loaves and fishes and put it back. Somehow, I could feel Jesus' eyes staring at me. *(pause)* Even though it had been a long journey and a longer time since I left home, I didn't feel hungry; at least not yet. Just as I had finished picking up my food, a man approached me, and he reached for my basket. At first, I pulled away, but the woman leaned toward me and said his name is Andrew and he was one of Jesus' disciples. She said, "Jesus must have need of your basket of food."

At first I was a little angry someone would take my lunch. I thought, *What am I going to eat?*

I watched as Jesus took my loaves and lifted one to the sky and gave thanks to God. Then he broke it and began passing the loaves to the men around him, and they began passing it out to the crowd. Likewise, He took my two fishes and blessed them, and He gave those out to other men who handed pieces of the fish to the crowd. I, too, was given a portion of the bread and the fish I had brought from home. *(pause)* I, like the rest of the people, began to eat, and I continued to watch as the food was passed out. Thinking, why have they not run out of food? It was only five small loaves and two tiny fish. Barely enough for me. Of course, my mother wanted to make sure I would not go hungry, but she did not give me so much it could feed a crowd like this. Can you imagine sharing your lunch with your whole school?

I thought to myself, this is a miracle. Just like the stories I heard of Jesus, healing the lame, the blind, those with diseases and the sick. *(Excited)* Feeding all those people with my little lunch. THAT was a miracle. *(Pause)* But wait, it wasn't over. When everyone was fed, Jesus said, "Gather up the fragments that remain, that nothing be lost." *(Pause)* Listen. Twelve! Twelve baskets were filled with the remains of the five barley loaves! How was that possible from my little lunch? A miracle! *(Pause)* I did not hear Jesus say much that day. I had gotten there too late to hear Him preach to the crowds. As the people began to proclaim Him for the miracle they had just witnessed, He departed and headed into the mountains, I guess, to be alone. I may have missed his preaching, but I was right on time to see the most amazing miracle of my life. *(Excited)* It was my lunch. *(Pause)*

Much happened after that. I soon realized that Jesus was much more than a miracle-maker; but a life-giver. Even as a young boy that day I began to understand that He came not to just do miracles, but to give us eternal life.

My family had heard the stories of Jesus feeding so many on that hillside that day, even before I arrived back home. But they could hardly believe it was my lunch that did it.

I tried to follow Him as often as I could. I remember sharing the words of Jesus with my family. "I am come that they might have life," He said, "and that they might have it more abundantly."

That day I accepted the words of Jesus and believed Him to be the Messiah and Savior; and I gave my heart and life to Him. As a young boy, I believed and trusted Jesus as the Christ, the living Son of God. You too, like me, can put your faith in Him, right now.

GIDEON'S SOLDIER

Costume(s) for Gideon's Soldier

Remember, Gideon's soldiers were not professionals but common farmers and shepherds.

Remember, Gideon's soldiers were not professionals but common farmers and shepherds.

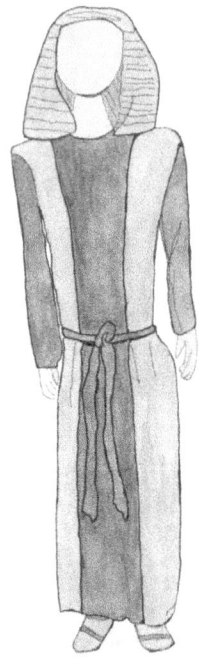

Remember, Gideon's soldiers were not professionals but common farmers and shepherds.

One of Gideon's Soldiers – Judges 7:1-22

The Scriptures:

¹Early in the morning, Jerub-Baal (that is, Gideon) and all his men camped at the spring of Harod. The camp of Midian was north of them in the valley near the hill of Moreh.

² The LORD said to Gideon, "You have too many men. I cannot deliver Midian into their hands, or Israel would boast against me, 'My own strength has saved me.'

³ Now announce to the army, 'Anyone who trembles with fear may turn back and leave Mount Gilead.'" So twenty-two thousand men left, while ten thousand remained.

⁴ But the LORD said to Gideon, "There are still too many men. Take them down to the water, and I will thin them out for you there. If I say, 'This one shall go with you,' he shall go; but if I say, 'This one shall not go with you,' he shall not go."

⁵ So Gideon took the men down to the water. There the LORD told him, "Separate those who lap the water with their tongues as a dog laps from those who kneel down to drink."

⁶ Three hundred of them drank from cupped hands, lapping like dogs. All the rest got down on their knees to drink.

⁷ The LORD said to Gideon, "With the three hundred men that lapped I will save you and give the Midianites into your hands. Let all the others go home."

⁸ So Gideon sent the rest of the Israelites home but kept the three hundred, who took over the provisions and trumpets of the others. Now the camp of Midian lay below him in the valley. ⁹ During that night the LORD said to Gideon, "Get up, go down against the camp, because I am going to give it into your hands.

¹⁰ If you are afraid to attack, go down to the camp with your servant Purah

¹¹ and listen to what they are saying. Afterward, you will be encouraged to attack the camp." So he and Purah his servant went down to the outposts of the camp.

¹² The Midianites, the Amalekites and all the other eastern peoples had settled in the valley, thick as locusts. Their camels could no more be counted than the sand on the seashore.

¹³ Gideon arrived just as a man was telling a friend his dream. "I had a dream," he was saying. "A round loaf of barley bread came tumbling into the Midianite camp. It struck the tent with such force that the tent overturned and collapsed."

¹⁴ His friend responded, "This can be nothing other than the sword of Gideon son

of Joash, the Israelite. God has given the Midianites and the whole camp into his hands."

¹⁵ When Gideon heard the dream and its interpretation, he bowed down and worshiped. He returned to the camp of Israel and called out, "Get up! The LORD has given the Midianite camp into your hands."

¹⁶ Dividing the three hundred men into three companies, he placed trumpets and empty jars in the hands of all of them, with torches inside.

¹⁷ "Watch me," he told them. "Follow my lead. When I get to the edge of the camp, do exactly as I do.

¹⁸ When I and all who are with me blow our trumpets, then from all around the camp blow yours and shout, 'For the LORD and for Gideon.'"

¹⁹ Gideon and the hundred men with him reached the edge of the camp at the beginning of the middle watch, just after they had changed the guard. They blew their trumpets and broke the jars that were in their hands.

²⁰ The three companies blew the trumpets and smashed the jars. Grasping the torches in their left hands and holding in their right hands the trumpets they were to blow, they shouted, "A sword for the LORD and for Gideon!"

²¹ While each man held his position around the camp, all the Midianites ran, crying out as they fled.

²² When the three hundred trumpets sounded, the LORD caused the men throughout the camp to turn on each other with their swords. *(NIV)*

The Preparation:

COSTUME – A shorter tunic with waist band and band around head

AGE – Could be any age. More likely middle age and older.

BACKGROUND – Simple person like a farmer or shepherd. No military experiences.

DEMEANOR – Willing and able to serve with Gideon and to serve God. A little worried about the small number of soldiers but has faith that the people of God will prevail.

The Story:

Many would call me a soldier. I am not. I am just a simple farmer; a simple shepherd. But I must admit I was in the most amazing battle ever recorded. Well, at least in my mind's eye I was. And there are those who would agree with me. It was a mighty battle.

What is my name? I was just one of many that day. My name was never mentioned in the Bible, but what we did that day as an army is a great account in God's Word.

However, I am a little ahead of my story.

I must go back seven years. God's people had forgotten what He had done for His people. As the story goes, God gave us into the hands of the Midianites, because of the evil we had done in the eyes of the Lord. Even my own father and our entire village had forsaken the Lord and turned to the worship of Baal. The control by Midian was so repressive, we had to flee to the mountains to hide in the caves, in clefts and other strongholds. As soon as our crops were planted, they would come and destroy the fields. Even our livestock was not spared. Our sheep, donkeys and cattle – nothing living was left alive. After seven years, we had become so impoverished, we finally turned to seek God's forgiveness and help.

It was at that time that God raised up a prophet to lead his people. Yet, like me, he was a simple man. He was thrashing wheat in a wine press, just to keep it hidden from the Midianites. It was at that moment that an angel appeared to Gideon and called him a "mighty warrior."

Those of us who knew Gideon all his life would have laughed at that! Gideon? A mighty warrior? *(Chuckle)* No way!

(Pause) Yet that is what he became.

We, the Israelites, had become so disheartened by the rule of the Midianites, we were ready to go to war. We had the numbers. When the call was sent out for an army to gather, 32,000 of us joined with Gideon. Thirty-two thousand! With an army that size, we could surely defeat the Midianites.

Why did I join you ask? Many in my family joined. Many of my friends and neighbors joined. With these numbers, we would win. We could claim victory for the people of Israel! We would return home as great warriors – like Gideon! That was our plan.

(Pause) But, that was not God's plan. Gideon told us that God said, "You have too many men."

What? Can any army have "Too many men?"

Gideon said to us, "Anyone who trembles with fear may turn back and leave this place."

I thought to myself, *No one will leave. This is for Israel! For our people! To protect our lives from tyranny!*

I was wrong. Twenty-two thousand turned tail and ran! I was shocked! How could they leave us like that?

Then Gideon told us the reason. He said God declared he could not deliver the enemy into our hands or we could boast against God and claim "Our own strength saved us." Humm, he had a point.

Let's see, what's left? *(Pause)* Ten thousand. Ten thousand left to defeat the enemy. Well, with God on our side, ten thousand could win, maybe. Maybe with a surprise attack. Or with spies to infiltrate the enemy camp, or maybe Gideon has some advanced military weapon that we could use to defeat the Midianites. Yes, with ten thousand men willing and able to fight, and God's help of course, we just might still win.

(Pause) I spoke too soon. The Lord tells Gideon, "There are still too many men."

What? OK, maybe a couple hundred might still be a little scared and we need to get rid of them. Scared ones could never help in battle. Good decision. So, Gideon did a strange thing. He sends us all to the riverbank – to take drink.

(Pause) OK. So, we all traveled to the river and got a nice drink of water. I reached down, cupped a handful of water and lapped it out of my hands. As I looked around, most of the other soldiers were on their knees.

Once we were full of water, Gideon announced, "Those who cupped with their hands, stand on this side of me."

As a good soldier, I obeyed.

Then Gideon announced, "The rest of you - go home."

(Confused face. Pause) What? I watched as most of the remaining army marched back to their homes. It was much easier to count how many remained than how many left.

(Pause. Shocked face.) Three hundred. THREE HUNDRED! *What kind of army is that?* I thought. *We are going to be slaughtered!*

I guess I could have looked on the bright side – *(Sarcastic)* now we have more provisions and more trumpets to use! However, that did not give me the best of feelings.

(Pause) Of course, Gideon was very brave. He actually went into the Midianite camp that night and returned with an amazing declaration - "Get up! The Lord has given the Midianite camp into your hands." I was happy to hear that, Now I said to myself; *Where are the weapons we will use?*

He divided us into three companies of one hundred each and gave each one of us a trumpet and an empty jar with torches inside. *(Confused.)* Did you hear that? A trumpet and an empty jar. What kind of weapons of war was that? They are going to have swords and shields and we will have trumpets and clay jars. Go figure. *(Sarcastic.)* Oh, I forgot. We had torches in the jars. That'll scare the enemy. *(Pause. Slowly.)* We are going to die.

Then Gideon said, ""Follow my lead. When I get to the edge of the camp, do exactly as I do. When I and all who are with me blow our trumpets, then from all around the camp blow yours and shout, 'For the Lord and for Gideon.'"

Gideon and the hundred men with him reached the edge of the camp at the beginning of the middle watch, just after they had changed the guard. We were to blow our trumpets and break the jars that were in our hands. That's what we did. The three companies blew the trumpets and smashed the jars. Grasping the torches in our left hands and holding the trumpets in our right hands, we blew and shouted, "A sword for the Lord and for Gideon!" While each of us held our position around the camp, all the Midianites ran, crying out as they fled.

When the three hundred trumpets sounded, the Lord caused the men throughout the Midianite camp to turn on each other with their swords and fight themselves.

God's victory was won! A trumpet and a clay jar. Who would have thought? I was there. Had I not been there I couldn't have believed it. I was allowed to see God win a might battle. Is there any way this army of only three hundred could claim the victory was ours? Ten thousand? Maybe. Thirty thousand? Of course. But three hundred? This victory was God's and God's alone.

So, what's the lesson I've learned? God's ways are not always our ways. You might say, His ways are a lot better than our ways. Allow God to lead you, no matter the path. Trust Him to deliver you from your battles and to bless you in all you do.

Look not to your own understanding but seek His face and His ways. I'm glad I did. Was I afraid? I was a lot braver when we had the thirty thousand. I was more afraid when we only had three hundred. I really had nothing to fear. God was and is in control.

Be of good courage. God is on your side and with you all the time.

THE INN KEEPER AND HIS WIFE

Costume(s) for Innkeeper and His Wife

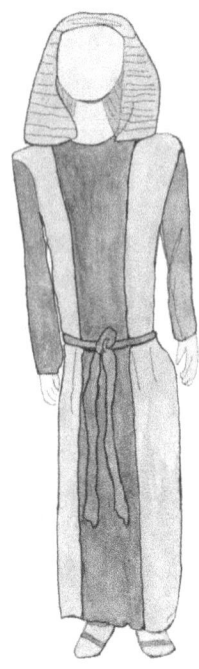

Plain costume of businessman with some color

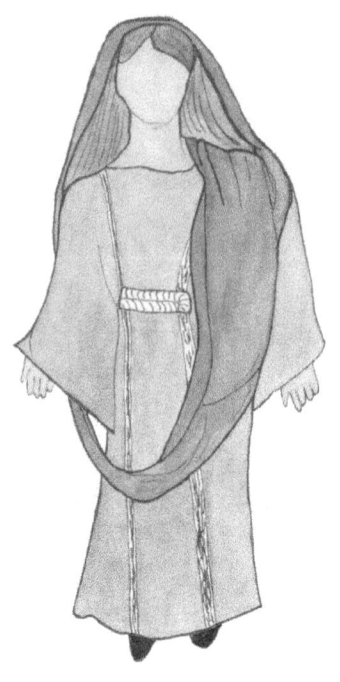

Plain costume of businessman's wife with some color and style

Plain costume of businessman with some color

Plain costume of businessman's wife with some color and style

The Inn Keeper and his Wife – Luke 2:1-7

The Scripture:

[1]In those days Caesar Augustus issued a decree that a census should be taken of the entire Roman world.

[2] (This was the first census that took place while Quirinius was governor of Syria.) [3] And everyone went to their own town to register.

[4] So Joseph also went up from the town of Nazareth in Galilee to Judea, to Bethlehem the town of David, because he belonged to the house and line of David. [5] He went there to register with Mary, who was pledged to be married to him and was expecting a child.

[6] While they were there, the time came for the baby to be born,

[7] and she gave birth to her firstborn, a son. She wrapped him in cloths and placed him in a manger, because there was no guest room available for them. *(NIV)*

The Preparation:

COSTUME – He should wear a tunic and an over-jacket with head covering and sandals. She should wear a tunic and long scarf to cover head and sandals.

AGE – Middle age or older

BACKGROUND – Both are fairly well-to-do. Not poor nor shabby, yet not fancy garments

DEMEANOR – They are a typical married couple who tend to argue over money.

The Story:

(The innkeeper and his wife begin at the back of the church and walk together down the aisle toward the front of the audience. They begin talking as soon as they start walking; complaining to each other until they arrive in the front. Angry faces.)

Innkeeper: What do you mean? I overcharge! I have a fair price!

Wife: You call that a "fair price?"

Innkeeper: Of course! I have expenses, you know!

Wife: Ha! Expenses? When is the last time you painted? And the steps! They are still broken. And the handrail! You said you would build one years ago! And has it been done? NO-O-O-O!

Innkeeper: Well, if I could charge a reasonable price, I could afford to get all those repairs done!

Wife: *(Meanwhile, the Wife has noticed the audience and tries to interrupt her husband.)*

Innkeeper: I mean you think all those materials are cheap? And the labor costs! Through the roof! *(Notices wife trying to get his attention.)* What? Why are you always interrupting me?

Wife: *(Tries to be hush-hush and private)* Husband, have you not noticed the people. I think they want to hear our story.

Both: *(Turn toward audience and change faces from angry to big grins at the same time.)*

Innkeeper: *(Very syrupy)* Hello! We are very pleased to be here and to share our story with you.

Wife: (Same syrupy) Oh, yes, we are happy, happy, happy, right husband?

Innkeeper: Yes. Happy, happy, happy!

Both: *(Pause; freeze with the same big grins on faces.)*

Wife: *(With same grin)* Aren't you going to tell the story, husband?

Innkeeper: *(With the same grin)* Oh, yes. I almost forgot.

Both: *(Release grins to normal faces.)*

Innkeeper: Our story starts with a young couple seeking shelter at my inn one evening. Now, you have to realize, the town was packed! The Roman Emperor, Caesar, had decreed that everyone, and I mean everyone, had to return to their town to be counted in the census. Well, the people who got here early - got the rooms. The late comers? They just missed out . . .

Wife: Wait just a minute here! Is that the attitude you take with our late arriving guests? Are you telling me the reason you turned away that young woman, a very pregnant young woman I might add; is because they were running a little late?

Innkeeper: *(flushed with embarrassment and trying to get a word in edgewise.)*

Wife: And where did you send them? Can you tell our friends here? Where EXACTLY did you send them?

Innkeeper: *(Stuttering)* Well, the, uh, well, uh the stable . . . .

Wife: *(Interrupts defiantly)* In the stable! He sent them to a smelly, dark, damp and crowded if I might add, STABLE!

Innkeeper: I'm sorry! I just didn't have enough room. I mean . . .

Wife: *(Interrupts)* My, my! That never seemed to matter when your entire family decided to show up during the Passover last year! You certainly made room for them!

Innkeeper: But wife, I . . .

Wife: I don't want to hear it! *(To the audience)* I said to my husband, 'You march yourself down to that stable this instant and tell that young, pregnant woman and her husband they are welcome to come in this inn.'

Innkeeper: But . . .

Wife: And – *(Tap fingertips)*

Innkeeper: *(To audience)* I did what she told me. I made my way down to the stable *(Looks at wife)* and I had every intention of inviting them back to the inn;

(Back to audience) but before I could even see them, *(Begin soft smile)* I could hear the soft, sweet whimper of a newborn baby. It stopped me in my tracks. I knew I was too late. The baby was already born in that stable. My wife was right - it was damp and dirty and cold - and very smelly. I didn't know what to do. As I knelt there, feely bad in the darkness, I got the scare of my life.

Wife: Sorry, I was just wondering what was taking you so long.

Innkeeper: Out of nowhere, she creeps up behind me and taps me on my shoulder!

Wife: Well, I didn't want to be too loud.

Innkeeper: I nearly jumped out of my skin. If I had yelled out, I would have scared that family – maybe even woken the baby! *(To wife)* And it would have been your fault!

Wife: Well, if you had let them stay at the inn in the first place, you wouldn't have been in that predicament!

Innkeeper: Before we could even start to argue, we heard a noise.

Wife: Yes, a noise!

Innkeeper: We thought it was soldiers.

Wife: Roman soldiers!

Innkeeper: But it wasn't soldiers.

Wife: No, it wasn't soldiers!

Innkeeper: *(Glances at wife for repeating him)*

Wife: *(Sheepishly smiles back)*

Innkeeper: *(Looks back at audience)* It wasn't soldiers. It was Shep . . . .

Wife: *(Starts to repeat husband)* It was shepherds! Shepherds! Who had been out on the hills tending their sheep, and they were so excited! They were a lot louder than us. *(Looks to husband)* Did I say they were excited?

Innkeeper: Yes wife, you said they were excited. *(Back to audience)* They claimed they had heard . . .

Wife: *(Interrupts)* Angels! Lots of angels! And they were singing! Singing angels! The shepherds said the angels were praising God and singing 'Glory to God and peace on earth'

Innkeeper: But one angel told them about the child. That angel said . . . .

Wife: *(Interrupts)* 'There is a baby born, right in our town, who is Christ the Lord!

Innkeeper: And the angel said . . .

Wife: *(Interrupts)* "You will find the baby wrapped in swaddling clothes lying in, get this, *(Very excitedly)* lying in a manger!'

Innkeeper: *(Starts to talk, but is interrupted again)*

Wife: It was our manger! *(Pause)* and, He was wrapped in - swaddling clothes!

Innkeeper: So it seems He was supposed to be born there.

Wife: Of course, He was supposed to be born there.

Innkeeper: It changed our lives.

Wife: It changed our lives.

Innkeeper: We became followers.

Wife: His Followers!

Innkeeper: We followed His life, even to the cross and to His resurrection. From then on, everything was different.

Wife: *(Slight pause)* Well, Husband, not everything.

Innkeeper: *(Questioning pause)* What do you mean? 'Not everything.'

Wife: *(Meekly)* Well, I feel like you still overcharge.

Wife and Innkeeper: *(Turn to walk out)*

Innkeeper: *(Begin walking back down aisle)* Me, Overcharge? I do not 'overcharge'!

Wife: *(Follows Husband back down aisle)* You could drop your prices some.

Innkeeper: I have expenses!

Both: *(Continue arguing until out of sight.)*

THE MAN WHO OWNED THE COLT

Costume(s) for Man Who Owned the Colt

Simple costume of farmer/shepherd.

Simple costume of farmer/shepherd.

Simple costume of farmer/shepherd.

The Man Who Owned the Colt - Mark 11:1-11; 15-17

The Scripture:

As they approached Jerusalem and came to Bethphage and Bethany at the Mount of Olives, Jesus sent two of His disciples,

² saying to them, "Go to the village ahead of you, and just as you enter it, you will find a colt tied there, which no one has ever ridden. Untie it and bring it here.

³ If anyone asks you, 'Why are you doing this?' say, 'The Lord needs it and will send it back here shortly.'"

⁴ They went and found a colt outside in the street, tied at a doorway. As they untied it,

⁵ some people standing there asked, "What are you doing, untying that colt?"

⁶ They answered as Jesus had told them to, and the people let them go.

⁷ When they brought the colt to Jesus and threw their cloaks over it, He sat on it.

⁸ Many people spread their cloaks on the road, while others spread branches they had cut in the fields.

⁹ Those who went ahead and those who followed shouted,

"Hosanna!"

"Blessed is He who comes in the name of the Lord!"[b]

¹⁰ "Blessed is the coming kingdom of our father David!"

"Hosanna in the highest heaven!"

¹¹ Jesus entered Jerusalem and went into the temple courts. He looked around at everything, but since it was already late, He went out to Bethany with the Twelve.

¹⁵ On reaching Jerusalem, Jesus entered the temple courts and began driving out those who were buying and selling there. He overturned the tables of the money changers and the benches of those selling doves,

¹⁶ and would not allow anyone to carry merchandise through the temple courts.

¹⁷ And as He taught them, He said, "Is it not written: 'My house will be called a house of prayer for all nations'? But you have made it 'a den of robbers.'" (NIV)

The Preparation:

COSTUME – Simple, plain costume with no frills nor much color. Tunic with a cloak and simple headpiece and sandals.

AGE – Older person who could have had young children.

BACKGROUND – Simple peasant/farmer/herder.

DEMEANOR – Very contrite and sorrowful for the errors of his ways and grateful for the forgiveness he has received.

The Story:

The colt belonged to me. At least at first it did, then it didn't then it did later. What I mean is, well, let me tell you the story and then I think you will understand. In the story someone owned the colt. It was mine in the beginning. Well, at first it belonged to a neighbor and then it was something I had saved money to buy for a long time. It was young and no one had ever ridden it before.

(Look confused) I've probably confused you. My name is not mentioned in the Bible. Not much is mentioned about me at all. But the colt. Now, that is a different story. I'm just a simple peasant, a farmer/ sheep herder from the hills outside of Jerusalem. I did whatever I could to earn money and provide for my family. At times I did some business with, uh, how should I say it? Men with less than honorable intentions. At the time I felt it was harmless. I needed the money and it allowed me to buy the colt. I had convinced myself that those people were rich and did not need the money. I was wrong of course. I wound up owing money to some very bad people and when I couldn't pay up, I met with some severe consequences.

The colt was for my son and daughter. I wanted them to have something I never had as a child. My ill-gotten gains had gone to buy that colt. They threaded my family if I didn't pay my debt. Instead they decided to take my colt.

I followed them into the city, hoping somehow to regain the animal. It was the week of Passover and the crowds were stifling. I realized that Jesus was headed to the entrance of the city and the crowd it caused was unbelievable.

I followed the men to the gate of the city, and I watched from afar as they tied the colt to a post. I could tell they were arguing about something. Probably about the colt, I'm sure. Then I noticed other men approach the colt, untie it and begin to walk away. Words were exchanged then, incredibly, they gave the colt away. I was stunned. I was furious. I could not believe what I did next. I ran up to the men who had taken the colt and yelled, "Why are you taking the colt away! You paid nothing for it!"

The men looked at one another before one answered, "Just like we told the others, the Lord needs it and will send it back here shortly."

I followed the men and watched them put cloaks on the colt and then I a saw a man be lifted to sit on the colt. As others flocked around, I asked a passerby, "Who are those people?"

"That's Jesus on the colt and the men around Him are His disciples." Someone said, racing by me with palm branches in his hands.

'Jesus? On my colt?' I thought to myself. *Only Kings enter a city riding on a colt. Is this the King we have been waiting for?*

I decided to follow Him as did many, many others. It was maddening. The yelling, the singing the masses in adoration to Jesus as He entered the city. Bodies were being pressed against me in the crowd. People yelling, "Hosanna!"

"Blessed is he who comes in the name of the Lord!"

"Blessed is the coming kingdom of our father David!"

"Hosanna in the highest heaven!"

I was being pushed along, but it didn't matter. I wanted to see what was going to happen, but I got lost in the crowd. I promised myself I would be back the next day.

I don't know what started it but a giant commotion was going on at the temple just as I arrived. I could see people who seemed to be running for their lives, I saw tables being thrown about and coins being flung far and wide. People were scrambling to pick up as many coins as they could. Then I heard a voice and there I could see Jesus exclaiming, "Is it not written: 'My house will be called a house of prayer for all nations'? But you have made it 'a den of robbers.'"

By this time, I had almost forgotten about my colt. Everyone seemed amazed at the teaching of Jesus. I had heard of His miracles – His healing of the lame, the blind, lepers – but I had never considered He could heal my heart. I needed forgiveness of the sins I had committed. But what could I do?

I thought. Jesus was still in the city when I left the gates. To my surprise, there was the colt, tied up in the same place, just like he said. At that moment, I saw the bad men who had taken my colt. I was close enough to hear them speak.

"The colt is here, just like we were told. What do we do with it?"

"I don't want anything to do with it. Did you not see what Jesus did with the money changers? I don't want that to happen to us!"

"Just leave it," another said.

"Just leave it," they all agreed and walked out of the city.

I slowly approached the colt, petting his back, then running my fingers through its mane. I was thinking this was the colt Jesus rode into the city - riding victorious, like a king. Like the King He is. I heard voices approaching and I spun away, fearful those evil men had changed their minds and returned.

As I turned to glance behind me, I saw Jesus and His disciples leaving Jerusalem. He paused for a brief moment to look at the colt, then me. He nodded before he continued on.

The colt was again mine.

(Pause.) There is a great lesson to be learned here. Just like the colt again belongs to me, I now belong to Jesus. He later paid the price for me on the cross.

Later that same week, He was falsely accused, falsely tried and then crucified. I realize now he died for my sins and arose again to give me victory over death. Jesus died for your sins too. It doesn't matter what your life has become or what you have done. Jesus paid the price. Accept His forgiveness today. Make Him your Lord and King.

ONE WHO HELPED THE PARAPLEGIC MAN

Costume(s) for One Who Helped the Paraplegic Man

Simple costume of farmer/shepherd.

Simple costume of farmer/shepherd.

Simple costume of farmer/shepherd.

One Who Helped the Paraplegic Man – Luke 2:1-12

The Scripture

¹ A few days later, when Jesus again entered Capernaum, the people heard that He had come home.

² They gathered in such large numbers that there was no room left, not even outside the door, and He preached the word to them.

³ Some men came, bringing to Him a paralyzed man, carried by four of them.

⁴ Since they could not get him to Jesus because of the crowd, they made an opening in the roof above Jesus by digging through it and then lowered the mat the man was lying on.

⁵ When Jesus saw their faith, He said to the paralyzed man, "Son, your sins are forgiven."

⁶ Now some teachers of the law were sitting there, thinking to themselves, ⁷ "Why does this fellow talk like that? He's blaspheming! Who can forgive sins but God alone?"

⁸ Immediately Jesus knew in His spirit that this was what they were thinking in their hearts, and He said to them, "Why are you thinking these things?

⁹ Which is easier: to say to this paralyzed man, 'Your sins are forgiven,' or to say, 'Get up, take your mat and walk'?

¹⁰ But I want you to know that the Son of Man has authority on earth to forgive sins." So, he said to the man,

¹¹ "I tell you, get up, take your mat and go home."

¹² He got up, took his mat and walked out in full view of them all. This amazed everyone and they praised God, saying, "We have never seen anything like this!" *(NIV)*

The Preparation:

COSTUME – Simple costume with tunic, over-jacket, belt, sandals and head piece

AGE – From younger adult to older man

BACKGROUND – Simple businessman in the town. Nothing fancy yet, nice clothes

DEMEANOR - Very much an unbeliever/doubter in the beginning but becomes a believer toward the end of the story.

The Story:

How many friends do you have? I mean REAL friends. To be honest, I had no REAL friends. Oh, I had acquaintances. People I knew and people who knew me, but no REAL Friends. Of course, this is at the beginning of my story. My name is not given in the Bible; but I was there; and my name is not that important. But my story? It was an amazing event in the Bible about which many people have read. Many pastors have preached about it too. Let me tell you my story.

Did I know Jesus? Not really. I had heard about Him. I had heard about His miracles and healings, about his claims and his teachings; but I did not KNOW Him.

I lived in a town named Capernaum. I'm sure you've heard of it. It wasn't a large city but a small one where almost everyone knew everyone else. I was acquainted with most of the people who lived there. I was told that Jesus had come to our town and was preaching and healing at a nearby home. I was curious to see Him and maybe experience seeing Him heal someone – but I wasn't sure of it. As I stood outside of the house, I could not find a way inside. All the window and doors were blocked with people, three- and four-deep. I didn't feel like fighting the crowds, so I had turned and began heading back home, thinking *Maybe another day.*

As I arrived back to the middle of town, I noticed several men had gathered around the local beggar who was always asking for money. He had been lying there so long, most people just ignored him and passed him by without another thought. But these three men were in deep conversation with him and it piqued my curiosity.

They soon noticed me approaching and motioned me closer.

"Sir, can you help us?" one called out to me.

I wasn't interested in getting involved, but I was interested in what was going on.

"No," I answered. "I was on my way home, and I'm late already." I lied. I wasn't late for anything.

"But sir," another pleaded. "We need you."

No one ever needed me. I listened.

"There is a man here in our town. He cannot walk, and he has been this way since birth. Jesus is near and we want to bring this man to see Him. Three of us cannot do it alone, we must have another to help.

"You'll never see this Jesus. I was just there, and all the windows and the doors are packed with curious people, hoping to get a glimpse of some miracle. You might want to try another day." I then turned and began to walk away.

"Please, we need you."

"Look," I answered. "It'll be a waste of time. You'll just have to bring him back and sitting up in that corner again. What would you have accomplished?" Again, I turned away.

"We believe Jesus can heal him."

Now I was intrigued. "You honestly believe you can get Jesus to heal him? He's been like this all his life. You think Jesus can just tell him to get up and pick up his blanket and walk?" I scoffed.

"No," one answered.

"There you go," I said. "So, what's the point? You'll be wasting your time – and my time."

Another spoke up, "No, we don't believe Jesus can only tell him to get up and walk, we believe Jesus can forgive him of his sins."

I paused for a moment trying to make sure I heard what I heard. "This I got to see."

I grabbed one corner of his bed and said, Let's go." Then I paused, "Since this Jesus is going to heal him," I mocked, "you won't need me to help bring him back, right?" Without a moment's hesitation, they all echoed, "Right."

The other three grabbed their corner and we began to walk to the house where Jesus was. I was a little surprised that He was still there. As I had told the three, the doorway and windows were overflowing with people trying to get a glimpse of what was happening inside. In fact, there are more now than when I passed earlier. There was no way those people were going to allow us to carry that man into the house to see Jesus. "See, I told you there was no way." I said. I then expected the three to pick up their corner and head on back. I knew I wasn't going to bring him back into town. I already told the three that.

"You said you wouldn't bring him back. Well, we still need you to help us get in the house. You did say you would help with that, right?"

Reluctantly, I agreed and asked "So, what's your plan? Drop him in from the roof?" I laughed. They didn't laugh.

I don't know how we managed, but with a lot of tugging and pulling, lifting, pushing and climbing, we got him to the roof and immediately the men began to pull away the tiles and supports, just enough to lower him into the middle of the house – right where Jesus was seated.

By now I was captivated by the events that were taking place.

When Jesus looked up, I could see His face. It was as if He could see right into their souls and see their faith. Then he looked at the paralyzed man and said something I wasn't expecting, but the others knew would happen. Jesus said to the paralyzed man, "Son, your sins are forgiven."

All of a sudden, an uproar was started in the house. Those who seemed to know the law were sitting there, mumbling, "Why does this fellow talk like that? He's blaspheming! Who can forgive sins but God alone?"

Immediately Jesus said, "Why are you thinking these things? Which is easier: to say to this paralyzed man, 'Your sins are forgiven,' or to say, 'Get up, take your mat and walk'? But I want you to know that the Son of Man has authority on earth to forgive sins." So, Jesus said to the man, " "I tell you, get up, take your mat and go home." I was shocked when I watched the man get up, take his mat and walk out as the crowd parted to let him out of the house. Everyone was amazed and they were praising God. "I have never seen anything like this!" I said to the others who were with me, but when I looked up, they had gone.

(Pause) It was just like they said. Jesus not only healed the man but forgave him of his sins. I never saw that paralyzed man again. He could walk now and probably never stopped walking. I'm sure he was telling the story about his healing, not only his body, but forgiveness of sin. As I climbed down from the roof, I realized I never got his name. As I landed on the ground I turned around and was face-to-face with Jesus. I was shocked and speechless all at the same time. He leaned into my face and very quietly, spoke these words; "Believe in me and your sins will be forgiven, and you shall have eternal life." That moment I became a believer, a follower, and my heart and life belonged to Him. I, like the paralyzed man I helped, would tell that story many times, and would see many people come to Jesus.

Have you met the Savior? Have you given your life to Him? Trust in his forgiveness and believe in His gift of eternal life.

THE OWNER OF THE UPPER ROOM

Costume(s) for Owner of the Upper Room

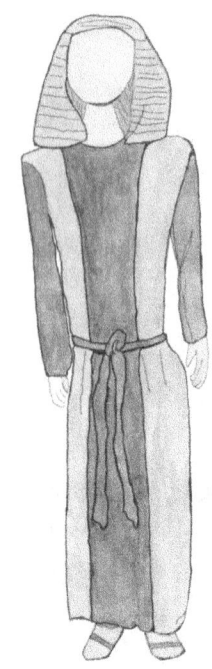

Fancier costume of businessman or
trader/ traveler

Fancier costume of businessman or
trader/ traveler

The Owner of the Upper Room - Matthew 26:17-19

The Scripture:

¹⁷ On the first day of the Festival of Unleavened Bread, the disciples came to Jesus and asked, "Where do you want us to make preparations for you to eat the Passover?"

¹⁸ He replied, "Go into the city to a certain man and tell him, 'The Teacher says: My appointed time is near. I am going to celebrate the Passover with my disciples at your house.'"

¹⁹ So the disciples did as Jesus had directed them and prepared the Passover. *(NIV)*

The Preparation:

COSTUME – This character, I believe, was someone who possessed a bit of wealth. So, his costume would be a tad better than most of the other characters in this book. Add a dash of color to his wardrobe.

AGE – any age, but most likely a little bit older to have had acquired any wealth and to own the upper room.

BACKGROUND – The story line indicates the owner was raised in a poor household but determined to become rich as an adult by any means he can.

DEMEANOR – He was very arrogant as a youth, but it was not until his encounter with Jesus, did he realize his sinful nature and it was then he repented and became a follower of Christ.

The Story:

You never learned my name, but I am the man who owned the upper room. I, personally, am quite insignificant in the story, but that room became a very significant part in the narrative of Jesus.

To own that upper room meant I had to be a somewhat wealthy man. And by all standards of that day, I was. It never started out that way. I began life as a son of a very, very poor father and mother. What my parents were able to scrape together, barely fed the family, and at times me and my siblings were required to work in various ways to put food on the table. My parents believed I came by my meager offerings through what they would call "legitimate means". I'm sad to say, it was far from the truth. I had learned early in life that I could do very well just stealing and cheating to earn money. It became my way of helping my family. I learned as I became older, those ways supported my lifestyle very comfortably. I did not enjoy the life of a poor son of poor parents; so, I decided to become - rich. I did whatever I could to gain money, to buy nice clothes, nice lodging – and - to acquire the upper room. Of all my properties, it was my favorite. It overlooked the main avenues into Jerusalem. I could see all that came and went in Jerusalem. As I stood on my balcony, I could see from the city's entrance to the temple itself. I felt like I had it all.

You see, the upper room had become a very profitable place. It was a prized location to hold many different types of functions. The Romans often rented the room to hold a variety of meetings. Some were military in nature. Some were boisterous parties that went well into the night. Some by the priests and temple leaders to make backroom deals, and some by individuals who did not want their identities known nor the purpose or content of their gatherings revealed. I didn't mind what happened as long as it meant money in my pocket.

But then one day, it all changed. My whole life changed, and the upper room changed as well. It was the week of Passover. The entire city was abuzz with visitors. My thoughts at the time was how much money I would be able to make renting out the upper room. I stood on my balcony viewing the masses of people as they flooded into the city and thronged along the streets passing multitudes of vendors with their hordes of goods who had lined the way. The streets and byways were a mass of people, pushing and shoving their way to and fro in the city. The yelling and screaming were music to my ears.

But then I hear a different sound. It was almost harmonious; not the wild voices of buying and selling and the bargaining that followed. Everyone's attention was being drawn to the entrance of the city. I could see palms being waved and cloaks being spread along the street approaching my room. I could see palm branches waved in the crowd and I strained my neck to see what was happening. Who was entering the city? Someone with this kind of fanfare obviously would need a place like my upper room to gather. Money, and lots of it, was dancing in my mind.

Wait, it looked like someone on a donkey, yes I could see it now. But the rider was not a king or some rich dignitary. It seemed like a common man, a simple peasant. Then as the procession passed beneath me, He looked up and our gaze was locked together. I had heard of a man called Jesus, but I had never seen Him. In that instant, I knew I must be eye-to-eye with Him. He continued to hold my stare as if He was drawing me to Himself. Much too quickly, our gaze was broken by the meandering streets and crowds of people chasing after Him.

I knew I had to see more. I raced out of my place and fought my way through the crowds. It mattered not who I had to brush aside to find this Jesus again. I did not find Him. The mass of humanity was much too thick to find a way through them. I went home, actually disappointed I could not meet Him.

The next day, Jesus returned to Jerusalem and again our eyes met. This time I felt I would see Him again.

The next day I heard a knock on my door. I was preparing to rent my room to the first group that desired it. During special festivals like this, many would be willing to pay a lot extra to secure my room for special events. As I open the door, I realized these were not any of my normal customers but some of the men I had seen with Jesus. Before I could speak, they at once said,

'The Teacher says: My appointed time is near. I am going to celebrate the Passover with my disciples at your house.'"

I was speechless. Jesus, in my house? How could I say no. Now would be my opportunity to meet Him and see him face-to-face.

"Yes, of course. My room is available. I would be overjoyed to have your Master dine here for the Passover."

As soon as I finished speaking, the men vanished into the crowd. I yelled out to them. "The fee. I forgot to tell you about the fee!"

I thought to myself, *Well, when they arrive to prepare for the Passover, then I'll tell them the cost of the room.*

Well the Passover happened. It was a very subdued affair, but then most of them are. However, this one seemed even more somber that others. I stood by to perform any service I could do to help with the Passover Feast and to find out who this man really was.

The more Jesus spoke, the more I realized the answer. Throughout the meal, He would cut a glance at me. His eyes seemed to pierce my heart and soul. His words spoke to me. I felt condemned yet full of hope at the same time. I could feel the weight of my guilt and fullness of forgiveness all at the same time. This man is the expected Messiah! He is the One we have been waiting for. I had not seen a miracle performed – no lame walking, no blind seeing, no deaf hearing. I never saw 5000 being fed with just two fish and a few loaves of bread. I could see me becoming a follower of Him. He had pulled me into His saving grace.

The change? My heart now belongs to Him. And the Upper Room? A meeting place for believers. A place of prayer and worship. A place of praise and forgiveness. Let Christ come into your life

THE RICH YOUNG RULER

Costume(s) for Rich Young Ruler

Fancier costume of businessman or trader/ traveler

Fancier costume of businessman or trader/ traveler

The Rich Young Ruler – Matthew 19:16-32

The Scripture:

[16] Just then a man came up to Jesus and asked, "Teacher, what good thing must I do to get eternal life?"

[17] "Why do you ask me about what is good?" Jesus replied. "There is only One who is good. If you want enternal life, keep the commandments."

[18] "Which ones?" he inquired.

Jesus replied, "'You shall not murder, you shall not commit adultery, you shall not steal, you shall not give false testimony, [19] honor your father and mother,'[c] and 'love your neighbor as yourself.'"

[20] "All these I have kept," the young man said. "What do I still lack?"

[21] Jesus answered, "If you want to be perfect, go, sell your possessions and give to the poor, and you will have treasure in heaven. Then come, follow me."

[22] When the young man heard this, he went away sad, because he had great wealth. *(NIV)*

The Preparation:

COSTUME -The costume for this character should be somewhat nice but not flashy. The hat should be turban-like. See the pictures in the appendix for a better idea.

AGE - This character can be at any age, but probably at least middle age. If younger, indicate in your presentation that this encounter with Christ, happened "recently" and "how could I ever forget it". If much older when making this presentation, you could state that this meeting with Jesus happened "many years ago" and it has stayed with you through many years.

BACKGROUND – The man was proud at the start. He is a man of statue, but he probably put more stock in his own status than he deserved.

DEMEANOR - Speak with a contrite voice. This character had met with Jesus and Jesus gave him little hope of acquiring salvation by his own efforts. However, as he considered what Jesus had said to him, he realizes the only hope he has will be to trust in Jesus and follow his commandments.

The Story:

You know who I am. You have read stories about me, but according to what you read in the Bible, it didn't end well. I'm not young anymore and I'm not rich anymore. Have you guessed yet? Correct, I am referred to as the "rich, young ruler". Well, I'm not a ruler anymore either. If I were not here to tell you my story, you would never recognize me at all.

Yes, I was young; at some point in my life, many years ago. And with that moniker, I was also very cocky. Did I mention I was very cocky? I believed I had the world on a string. And what made that ever more intolerable for those around me, I had a little change in my purse. I wasn't really rich, but hearing coins jangling in the belt around my waist not only made me feel rich, but also bolstered my arrogance. I had many friends, or so I thought, but that's getting ahead of my story.

I might have been referred to as a "man about town." I was in everyone's business. I knew who was selling and who was buying and when the goods would arrive. I wanted to be the first to know anything. If gossip was to be spread, I felt it was my obligation to spread it. Whatever was to be heard, I heard it first.

The most interesting tidbit circulating around town at the time, was about this new man around town named Jesus. I was told He was responsible for many healings and miracles. Everyone was calling Him "good".

Hummm. Well, I was good, too. So how would I stack up against this new man; this Jesus?

I met up with Jesus in Judea on the other side of the Jordan River. I heard Him being questioned about marriage and divorce. Hoo'hum. Not an issue with me - I was not married. Then I watched as the commoners would bring their little children to Jesus. His disciples rebuked Him, but He answered them by saying, "Let the little children come to me, and do not hinder them, for the kingdom of heaven belongs to such as these." As soon as he blessed the last on, I saw my chance to move in.

"Teacher, what good thing must I do to get eternal life?"

"Why do you ask me about what is good?" Jesus replied. "There is only One who is good. If you want enternal life, keep the commandments."

This is sounding too easy. "Which ones?" I inquired.

Jesus answered, "'You shall not murder, you shall not commit adultery, you shall not steal, you shall not give false testimony, honor your father and mother,' and 'love your neighbor as yourself.'"

A piece of cake, I thought. "All these I have kept," I gleefully answered. "What do I still lack?"

Jesus responded, "If you want to be perfect, go, sell your possessions and give to the poor, and you will have treasure in heaven. Then come, follow me."

Whoa! When did selling everything I have and giving it to the poor, come into this? I thought. Needless to say, I went away sad. You see, face it, I was rich.

Well, that's my story. It's right there in the Bible. The whole sad tale.

(Pause) Yes, that's the sad tale, but not the whole tale.

For some reason, Jesus had gotten under my skin. Had I really kept all the commandments? There are a few I can categorially say 'I have not broken that commandment!" Then there are a few where it might be a little borderline. Well, and a couple I must confess – I out-and-out lied.

For example, the false witness one. It was a little lie to the authorities, but it helped me to make a pretty good monetary gain, Well, quite a bit of monetary gain. And the honor your parent thing – I cheated them, and it helped me to become a little richer – well a lot richer.

For years I struggled with the words Jesus spoke to me. I could not cut myself apart from the riches I had acquired, and yet, my life had this nagging feeling I would never gain eternal life. And how would I be able to follow Him now, He's dead.

I had heard of Jesus' arrest, the trial, and His crucifixion. He didn't deserve to die. If anyone was good, it was Him.

Then I heard He rose from the dead, just like He said He would. Three days in a borrowed tomb.

By this time, I had no friends. They were only interested in me as long as I had money. Once the lean times began, they did not care for me anymore.

The words of Jesus never left me. As I watched the lives of those around me who were less fortunate than me, I began to feel an obligation to help them. Some were very grateful; others just took advantage. Yet I had a feeling I was beginning to follow what Jesus had said.

Then one night, I realized I was tired, very tired. I had nothing left, it was all gone. I hadn't spent it on myself. It was all gone - given away.

I now understand what Jesus meant. It was not the money that kept me out of Heaven, It was my unwillingness to share with those around me, yet something was still missing. It wasn't just my money Jesus was talking about. It was my unwillingness to give me – myself to Him. All this time I could have been living my life for Him. I just needed to accept His gift and give my heart to Him. Now I know I will have eternal like in Heaven – not because of what I have done, but what He has done for me.

SERVANT AT THE CANA WEDDING

Costume(s) for Servant at the Cana Wedding

Very plain costume of servant with little or no color

Very plain costume of servant with little or no color

Very plain costume of servant with little or no color

Servant at the Cana Wedding – John 2:1-12

The Scripture:

On the third day a wedding took place at Cana in Galilee. Jesus' mother was there, [2] and Jesus and His disciples had also been invited to the wedding. [3] When the wine was gone, Jesus' mother said to Him, "They have no more wine."

[4] "Woman,[a] why do you involve me?" Jesus replied. "My hour has not yet come."

[5] His mother said to the servants, "Do whatever He tells you."

[6] Nearby stood six stone water jars, the kind used by the Jews for ceremonial washing, each holding from twenty to thirty gallons.[b]

[7] Jesus said to the servants, "Fill the jars with water"; so they filled them to the brim.

[8] Then He told them, "Now draw some out and take it to the master of the banquet."

They did so, [9] and the master of the banquet tasted the water that had been turned into wine. He did not realize where it had come from, though the servants who had drawn the water knew. Then he called the bridegroom aside [10] and said, "Everyone brings out the choice wine first and then the cheaper wine after the guests have had too much to drink; but you have saved the best till now."

[11] What Jesus did here in Cana of Galilee was the first of the signs through which He revealed his glory; and his disciples believed in him.

[12] After this He went down to Capernaum with his mother and brothers and His disciples. There they stayed for a few days. *(NIV)*

The Preparation:

COSTUME – Simple, plain costume, with tunic, head piece, sandals and over coat.

AGE – Can be any adult age also can be performed by a man or a woman with minor alterations.

BACKGROUND – Common person

DEMEANOR – Overjoyed with the remembrance of the miracle Jesus performed.

The Story:

Anybody been to a wedding lately? I have, well, not lately. *(Look up quickly to someone in the back.)* What's that? When? Ok, about *(Pause)* 2,000 years ago. But

I remember it as if it was yesterday. Weddings. Back then they were very different from today.

Have you ever been to a wedding that lasted three to five hours? How about three to five DAYS! days? Probably not. But weddings back in that time always did.

It's a wedding like that I want to talk to you about today. It started out like every other wedding. Every community, when a wedding was to be celebrated, would select the Master of the Feast. It was an important position. He would be responsible for planning the whole event. It was an honor to be selected and if anything at the party would be amiss, it would a great embarrassment to the Master. He would spend a great amount of time to make sure every preparation was carried out to the last detail. Adequate space for a grand party, enough food and wine for everyone; music for the entertainment. And remember, there had to be enough for every guest for up to five days! It was a daunting task.

I must admit, weddings were a wonderful and fun event. Even though I was always a servant, I still had a good time. The festivities would begin usually on Wednesday; in most cases, at midnight. The whole community would gather and begin the march from the house of the groom and with his family and friends, the procession would continue to the house of the bride. It was a noisy and boisterous affair - loud voices, making jokes of all kind, speeches and expressions of goodwill to the bride and groom. The whole group would then move to the house of the groom where the festivities would be held.

As I told you, the whole community would be invited. And since Jesus was a part of this area of Galilee called Cana, He was invited too.

Of course, at that time, Jesus was just beginning His ministry. Not many people knew of Him. He was a carpenter's son. That's all most of us knew.

Along with his mother, Mary, His disciples were invited as well.

Later, there were those who had heard rumors of Jesus performing miracles. Some even claiming they were there and saw it happen. Mostly no one believed them. But at the wedding, many of us became believers that Jesus was a miracle maker.

I'm getting a little ahead of myself. Let me start from the beginning. *(Look up quickly to someone in the back.)* What's that? Who am I? Oh, I forgot to tell you. My name was never mentioned in the Bible. I was just one of the servants at that wedding feast. I had worked for the Master that day. As far as the Master was concerned, there were two items that was paramount to any feast like this – never run out of food; never run out of drink. Period.

My task? Keep the drink flowing for all the guests. It was a fairly easy job. Fill the pitchers from the large jars of wine, then fill the cups when they were empty. How hard can that be? Right?

(Look around at audience.) Now we had a trick. You always would start off pouring

the good stuff – the best wine first. That would impress the guests. Once everyone had drunk enough, you can go get the cheap stuff. *(Look around.)* Everyone did it. Nobody cared. And no one knew the difference.

But then disaster struck! Something no one counted on! The good wine was long gone, but then so was the cheap stuff! What could have happened? One of two things – we didn't make enough or the guests drank too much. This was a monumental disaster!

Who was going to tell the Master? *(Pause, sheepishly)* It was me.

As I walked up to the Master, I expected to be chewed out, maybe be even fired! But when I told him what had happened, he was much calmer than I thought he would be.

He said, "We had a much larger crowd here. I expected Jesus and a few of his friends to come, but all twelve? They're probably the reason we ran out. You go tell him to find more wine. Do it!" Then he just turned away.

At first, I didn't know what to say to Jesus and his friends. What if He said "no"? But then I saw His mother, Mary. I could ask her. Surely, He wouldn't refuse His mother.

There was some discussion I didn't understand at the time. Something about His time not come yet, or something like that. Then Mary said to me, "Do whatever He says."

Jesus had been staring at six of the stone water jars used for ceremonial washing. Each held twenty to thirty gallons of water. Even without water, they were very heavy. He said, "Fill the jars with water."

He watched as we poured pail after pail of water into each one. He didn't say a word until we had filled each one to the very top.

Then Jesus said, "Now draw some out and take it to the master of the banquet." Not one of the servants wanted to do that. *(Sigh.)* It fell to me again. So, I took a cup of the water and handed it to the master. I waited for him to spew it out and accuse me of trying to poison him. He didn't know where it came from, but all the servants knew it came from the water jars.

He then said the unexpected. He called the bridegroom, and stated, "Everyone brings out the choice wine first and then the cheaper wine after the guests have had too much to drink; but you have saved the best till now."

Best till now? I spoke under my breath. I ran back to the others. By the time I got back to the watering jugs, the rest of the servants had already began sipping the wine from the watering jars.

"It's wine!" they all exclaimed.

"Jesus had turned the water in to wine!" one cried out.

"It's a miracle!" another shouted.

I turned to see Jesus smiling at me. And I smiled back.

Over the years, I have had many questions about that wedding. "Did he really turn the water into wine?" Absolutely, I responded. Many also asked me, "Did Jesus stay at the wedding the whole time?" From what I remember, He did.

Another question I always get is, "Did Jesus dance?" *(pause, wide grin.)* Dancing was an important part of every wedding celebration. "But did Jesus dance?" they would ask again.

Dancing was a part of not only weddings, but of other celebrations as well. I'm sure Jesus attended many celebrations after that first wedding.

(Pause.) It was a minor miracle; changing water into wine. Later He healed many infirmities and diseases and changed many lives.

It wasn't just the miracle, but what that miracle meant.

You see, that water represents the old law, the outward ceremonial cleansing. Do good, keep the rules, go to the synagogue, read the Scripture, act with honor and integrity.

But the new wine represents Christ's life and death. We no longer need to trust in our own efforts, but we can trust in what Jesus did on the cross. His forgiveness comes without cost to us, but through His grace.

The good news for us is that the new wine will never, ever run out. He is the new wine in our lives. Accept Him as your Savior today. Trust to Christ for the forgiveness of your sins and for an eternity in Heaven with Him.

(Begin to walk away, they stop.) What? *(Emphatic.)* Did Jesus dance.? *(Smile broadly with a big laugh and continue to walk away.)*

SHEPHERD WHO HEARD THE ANGELS

Costume(s) for Shepherd Who Heard the Angels

This costume would be a very typical Bible Character outfit for a shepherd

This costume would be a very typical Bible Character outfit for a shepherd

This costume would be a very typical Bible Character outfit for a shepherd

This costume would be a very typical Bible Character outfit for a shepherd

Shepherd Who Heard the Angels – Luke 2:8-20

The Scripture:

[8] And there were shepherds living out in the fields nearby, keeping watch over their flocks at night.

[9] An angel of the Lord appeared to them, and the glory of the Lord shone around them, and they were terrified.

[10] But the angel said to them, "Do not be afraid. I bring you good news that will cause great joy for all the people.

[11] Today in the town of David a Savior has been born to you; He is the Messiah, the Lord.

[12] This will be a sign to you: You will find a baby wrapped in cloths and lying in a manger."

[13] Suddenly a great company of the heavenly host appeared with the angel, praising God and saying,

[14] "Glory to God in the highest heaven,   and on earth peace to those on whom His favor rests."

[15] When the angels had left them and gone into heaven, the shepherds said to one another, "Let's go to Bethlehem and see this thing that has happened, which the Lord has told us about."

[16] So they hurried off and found Mary and Joseph, and the baby, who was lying in the manger.

[17] When they had seen Him, they spread the word concerning what had been told them about this child,

[18] and all who heard it were amazed at what the shepherds said to them.

[19] But Mary treasured up all these things and pondered them in her heart.

[20] The shepherds returned, glorifying and praising God for all the things they had heard and seen, which were just as they had been told. *(NIV)*

The Preparation:

COSTUME – Wear a basic Bible costume with staff.

AGE – Middle age or older

BACKGROUND – Clothes are work clothes, not shabby but well used.

DEMEANOR – These are simple people who witnessed the birth of the Savior. Full of wonder.

The Story:

Are you going to ask me? *(Pause.)* Everyone asks me. *(Pause.)* Aren't you? *(Pause.)* Wait! You don't know who I am. I forgot to introduce myself. I was one of them. If you ask the others, they will claim they were first, but the truth be told, I was the first one there.

(Look out into the audience.) What's that? Oh, my name. Well, it's not mentioned in the Bible, and the Bible never mentions who was first, but you have to take my word for it; I was the first one there. I was just a shepherd – sheep herder. You have to watch sheep. People call sheep dumb. Well, I tend to disagree. They are not dumb. Sheep are helpless.

Since they have no horns, no claws and no sharp teeth, they cannot protect themselves. Why, they can't even outrun a predator. So, we watch them. Night and day, we watch them.

We were all shepherds from Bethlehem. Why, outside of Jerusalem, I've not been far from home my entire life. I just watched sheep.

(Pause.) But you didn't come to hear me talk about sheep You want me to tell you - the story. It's a story I have told a thousand times since that amazing night.

I'll start from the beginning. I didn't have to watch sheep every night. We would take turns. Some had the day shift; some had the night shift and we would change up and do the opposite. To be honest, no one really liked the night shift. It was the most dangerous shift, not only for the sheep but us shepherds as well. Of course, you couldn't sleep on the job. You had to stay awake. But that is not my story.

This is my story. That night I had the nightshift. The nights got cool. We would wrap up in blankets. It started out like every other night. – quiet and calm. Except for a random bleat every now and then, it was all silence.

(Pause.) That is, until the angels appeared. *(Pause.)* Yeah, angels. *(Pause.)* Did I mention angels appeared? I had never been so scared in my life. The Bible says we were "terrified". Now, if I could think of a stronger word than "terrified" I would use it.

First, it was just one angel. He said, "Do not be afraid. I bring you good news that will cause great joy for all the people."

Don't be afraid. Ha! If you think that kept us from being afraid, you have another thing coming.

But then the angel said something we could have never imagined, and this took our fear away. "Today in the town of David a Savior has been born to you; He is the Messiah, the Lord. This will be a sign to you: You will find a baby wrapped in cloths and lying in a manger." The Messiah? The Savior? Our Lord? Born here, in Bethlehem?

Before we could even think about finding Him, the whole sky lit up with angels, singing and praising God, saying,

"Glory to God in the highest heaven, and on earth peace to those on whom His favor rests."

And just as soon and they appeared in the sky, they were gone, disappeared, vanished.

We stood there, dumbfounded, staring at each other. Each of us wondering, *What just happened?* We began to talk, everyone speaking at the same time, and not one hearing what the other was saying.

Finally, someone yelled out, "Stop talking, all of you! Did you hear what the angel said? The long-awaited Messiah is finally here. Born right here in Bethlehem! Is not this the answer to prophecy?"

"But where is He?' cried out another. "How can we find Him?"

"He's in a manger?" another yelled out.

"A manger? In a stable manger?" one more questioned. "There are so many in Bethlehem. How can we find Him?"

It was me who finally spoke up." Let's go to Bethlehem and see this thing that has happened, which the Lord has told us about."

Without thinking, we left the sheep and ran towards town, and there in the distance, we saw the faint glow of a lantern, and as we approached the stable, we could hear the soft whimper of a baby, and there we found the mother, her name was Mary, and her husband Joseph and there in the manger was the baby. He was to be our Savior, our Messiah, our Lord.

She said, "His name is Jesus."

It mattered not it was the middle of the night, we had to spread the word. We knocked on every door we could in that small village. We shared all that we had seen and heard. Everyone, and I mean everyone, rejoiced and were amazed at what we had told them. No one slept after that. We went back that night continued to glorify and praise God for all we witnessed - the angels appearing and giving us the good news of our Savior being born in our town and we experienced His birth and celebrated His coming that night.

Have you seen angels? Have you heard them singing? Maybe, maybe not, but you can experience the joy of having Jesus in your life. You can experience the same joy and gladness we shepherds were a part of. Our lives were changed that night as we encountered the Christ, Jesus, who became our Lord and Savior. You can have your life changed even now as you give your heart to Him. Trust in Him to forgive your sins and to offer you an eternity in Heaven.

Oh, and the sheep? They did just fine while we were gone.

Thank you.

COMING SOON!
Ordinary People – Extraordinary God – Volume 2

This collection of monologues will include:

- Jesus Heals the Demon-Possessed Man
- The Healing at the Pool
- The Fortune-Telling Slave Girl
- The Woman at the Well
- A Centurion Believes in Jesus
- The Woman and the Alabaster Jar
- The Man with the Withered Hand
- Visitor from the East
- And more

Watch for the release date for this book and others written by Michael E. Owens on the following social media and websites:

- Website - www.booksbyMEO.com
- Book Orders - www.scribblersweb.com
- Facebook - @booksbymeo
- Twitter - @mikeandfriends2
- Facebook - @booksbyMEO
- Instagram – bookbyMEO
- Podcast - "The Mike and Friends 2 Show"

Patterns for Bible Costumes

If you are looking for patterns to sew Bible costumes, check out the following patterns which may be available at your local fabric shop or online:

McCall's #2339

McCall's #2060

Simplicity #4795

Other Titles Available from Michael E. Owens
Available from Scribblersweb.com and Amazon

The I Hate Vegetables Book of Poetry for Kids

The "I Hate Vegetables Book of Poetry for Kids" is a fun, whimsical and irreverent look at the veggies kids hate to eat the most. It's a book to be enjoyed by those who hate vegetables as well as those who love them! Please – read and be entertained! (and eat your veggies!)

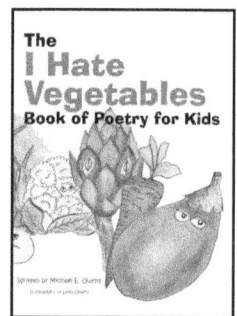

Does the River Ever End?

It's the 1840s along the Mississippi River and Mike Fink must live in the shadow of his infamous father, with no one giving him a fair shake. Mike and a slave, Cletus, believing they will be charged for two murders on the riverboat, escape capture through the backwoods of Illinois, down the Ohio and Mississippi Rivers, heading as far away from Cairo as they can. Being chased by the law and outlaws too, will Mike and Cletus finally make it to Memphis and freedom?

Summer of Heroes

In the 1870's, Billy was looking forward to a lazy summer in West Texas, waiting for his dad to return home to take their cattle to market. When he doesn't return, the task of trail boss lands in his lap. On his travels with the herd, he gains an unexpected trail hand and runs into a band of rustlers, the man the Chisholm trail is named after, Bass Reeves, the first black Texas Ranger, and a famous Indian chief. On his return home, he has another unexpected visitor and goes after his dream – a wild stallion in the hills. Billy never considered himself a hero, but others had a different idea.

Coming Soon!

Eggs! Eggs! Eggs!

Peter Rabbit is running short of painted Easter Eggs for all the good boys and girls. The forest animals, who paint the eggs, are beginning to become overwhelmed. Their new invention seems to be the answer until it is stolen by the Evil Woodsman. But thanks to the daffy Wood Fairy, everything turns out great! A wonderful musical for younger grades and special needs.

Santa Checks His List Around the World

Take a ride with Santa as he visits the children of the world, one country at a time. Egypt, Canada, Greece, Scandinavia, China, Ireland, Mexico and other countries too!